For Toby Hall
I.W.

For Beccy
A.R.

First published in Great Britain in 2002 by

GULLANE
CHILDREN'S BOOKS

Winchester House, 259-269 Old Marylebone Road,
London NW1 5XJ

1 3 5 7 9 10 8 6 4 2

Text © Ian Whybrow 2002
Illustrations © Adrian Reynolds 2002

The right of Ian Whybrow and Adrian Reynolds
to be identified as the author and illustrator of this work
has been asserted by them in accordance with the
Copyright, Designs and Patents Act, 1988.

A CIP record for this title is available from the British Library.

ISBN 1 86233 415 3

Printed and bound in Belgium

Romp *in the* Swamp

Written by **Ian Whybrow**

Illustrated by **Adrian Reynolds**

GULLANE
CHILDREN'S BOOKS

Mum and Nan were taking Sam to see her new school. That was why Harry and the dinosaurs had to go and play with some girl called Charlie.

Harry called their names but
the dinosaurs were hiding.

"Don't let Charlie play with us, Harry," said Apatosaurus.
"She might do bending on our legs," said Anchisaurus.
"She might chew our tails," said Triceratops.
"She won't understand about dinosaurs," said Scelidosaurus.

"Don't worry," said Harry. "You get in the bucket.
I won't let anyone else play with *my* dinosaurs."

"What took you so long, slowcoach?" said Sam.
"None of your business!" said Harry.
Good thing Nan sat between them.

Charlie and her mum came to the door to meet Harry.
Harry hid the dinosaurs behind his back.

"Goodbye!" called Mum. "Have a good time!"
Harry and the dinosaurs didn't think they would.

Charlie went inside and
sat on the sofa with her toys.

Harry sat at the other end of the sofa.
He guarded the dinosaurs and wouldn't speak.

Then Charlie went off
and found a big basket.
In went her dumper truck
and her tractor.

In went some cushions,
in went some boxes.

In went some pans
and some plants and
some string.

Harry and the dinosaurs
followed her into the garden.
"What is she doing?"
whispered Harry.

"She's making a primeval forest!" said Anchisaurus.
"And a primordial swamp!" said Triceratops.
"That looks fun!" said Stegosaurus.

"Hissssss"

went the hose like a great big snake.

"Look out!" Harry shouted.
"That snake might bite us!
Oh no, he's squeezing
Tyrannosaurus!
Quick! Save him!"

Harry and the dinosaurs joined in the noisy game.
Anchisaurus went crash with the tractor.
Scelidosaurus went bump with the dumper truck.
Apatosaurus and Triceratops made a strong
snake-lead out of string.
Stegosaurus grabbed the snake's tail.

"Help me with the snake cage!" shouted Charlie.
Whump went the snake cage and
captured the snake!

"**Raaaah!**"
said Tyrannosaurus.
"You can't catch me,
Mister Snaky!"

Then everyone did a noisy capture-dance.

"Hooray!" said Charlie. "What shall we do now?"
"Let's all have a feast!" said Harry.

"Would you like to play with
Charlie another day?" called Mum.
"Definitely!" said Harry.
"Definitely!" said the dinosaurs.

ENDOSAURUS